Nicky and the Twins

The Lost Rabbit

First published in hardback in Great Britain by
HarperCollins Publishers Ltd in 1997
1 3 5 7 9 10 8 6 4 2
ISBN 0 00 198120-X (HB)

First published in Picture Lions in 1997
1 3 5 7 9 10 8 6 4 2
ISBN 0 00 664511-9 (PB)

Picture Lions is an imprint of the Children's Division,
part of HarperCollins Publishers Ltd, 77-85 Fulham Palace Road,
Hammersmith, London W6 8JB
Text copyright © Tony Bradman 1997
Illustrations copyright © Susan Winter 1997
The author and illustrator assert the moral right to be identified
as the author and illustrator of this work.
A CIP catalogue record for this book is available from the British Library.
Printed and bound in Singapore by Imago

Nicky and the Twins

The Lost Rabbit

Tony Bradman & Susan Winter

PictureLions
An Imprint of HarperCollins*Publishers*

Nicky was feeling rather nervous.

Mum and Dad were taking her to the dentist for a check-up, and the prospect was making her go quite fluttery inside.

This was a job for her old rabbit, Mr Bob, Nicky decided.

Now why was he in the Twins' toy box?

But Nicky's teeth were fine, and visiting the dentist turned out to be fun!

In fact, Nicky relaxed
such a lot... she forgot
Mr Bob.

"Does this belong to you?" said the lady
receptionist.
The Twins seemed pleased to see him, too.

A few days later, Nicky was feeling rather nervous again. She was going to stay the night at Granny's house... without Mum and Dad!

This was a job for Mr Bob,
Nicky decided.

Now why was
he in the Twins'
cupboard?

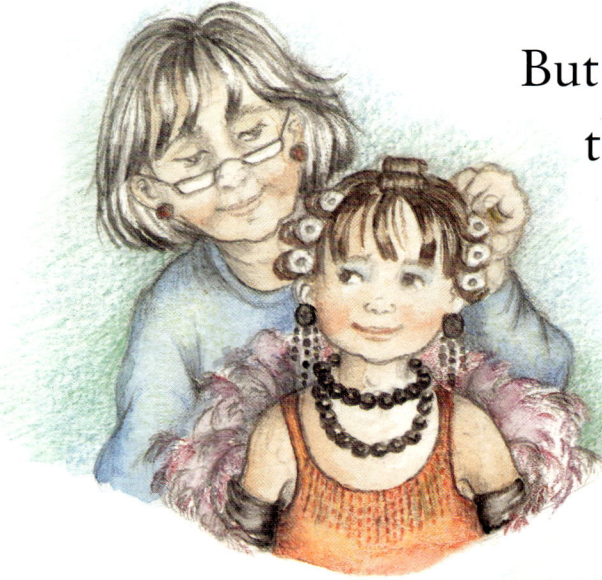

But Nicky had a terrific time with her Here's-What-We'll-Do, Peek-a-Boo Granny.

In fact, Nicky relaxed such a lot... she forgot Mr Bob.

"Hang on," Granny yelled. "You've left someone behind!"

The Twins stopped yelling then, as well.

A few days later, Nicky was feeling rather nervous again. Everyone at ballet class had to dance alone for all the Mums and Dads!

This was a job for Mr Bob, Nicky decided.

Now why was he in the Twins' drawer?

But Nicky did a wonderful dance, and
Mrs Tyson said she was the star of the
show. In fact, Nicky relaxed such a lot...
she forgot Mr Bob.

"Yours, I believe!" Mrs Tyson called.
The Twins seemed very relieved.

A few days later,
Nicky was feeling
rather nervous again.

She had been invited
to a special tea at her
friend Anna's house.
Nicky was worried.
She didn't know what to wear.

This was a job for Mr Bob, Nicky decided. Now why was he in the Twins' bedside cabinet?

But Nicky enjoyed
herself more than she
had ever done before.
In fact, she relaxed
such a lot... she
forgot Mr Bob.

But the Twins certainly
didn't, oh no... they hugged
and hugged him, and wouldn't
let him go.

A few days later, Nicky was feeling rather nervous again. Mum and Dad were taking her to the clinic for her pre-school booster.

This was *definitely* a job for Mr Bob, Nicky decided.

Now why was he
in the Twins' bed?

But Nicky found out she didn't have much
to worry about. In fact, the booster hurt,
but not a lot, so
she relaxed...
and forgot
Mr Bob.

"I don't think he wants
a jab, does he?" laughed
the doctor,

and the Twins certainly seemed to agree!

That night, Nicky kept an eye on the Twins...
and on Mr Bob.

Everywhere that Mr Bob went, the Twins
were close behind.

The Twins loved Mr Bob, Nicky realised,

and she knew she didn't mind.

A few days later, Nicky felt rather nervous again. She was going to school for the very first time, and she felt quite fluttery inside. But she didn't need Mr Bob, she'd decided.

No, Nicky had another job for him...

...staying at home to look after the Twins!